To my dear husband Michael, whose love, support, and fine editing skills made this book possible. Thank you for supporting all my zany endeavors, for believing in me, trusting me, and for infusing our lives with spiritual meaning.

AuthorHouse™ LLC
1663 Liberty Drive
Bloomington, IN 47403
www.authorhouse.com
Phone: 1-800-839-8640

Published by AuthorHouse 08/29/2014

ISBN: 978-1-4969-3521-2 (sc)
ISBN: 978-1-4969-3522-9 (e)

Any people depicted in stock imagery provided by Thinkstock are models,
and such images are being used for illustrative purposes only.
Certain stock imagery © Thinkstock.

This book is printed on acid-free paper.

Because of the dynamic nature of the Internet, any web addresses or links contained in this book may have changed
since publication and may no longer be valid. The views expressed in this work are solely those of the author and do not
necessarily reflect the views of the publisher, and the publisher hereby disclaims any responsibility for them.

authorHOUSE®

Lessons from Pony School

Superpony Me!

CHAYA (AGE 9), SHAINDEL (AGE 9)
AND NINA GREENE

Miss Bells

The most wonderful
Ponyschool teacher!

Gooseberry

Responsible, helpful
and a good friend

Clover

Outgoing
and creative

Buttercup

Shy and content

Prancer

The eldest, wisest pony

Dandy

Lively and full of mischief

Poppy

Sensitive and loyal

1

The Pony School triangle rang and all the ponies rushed to their places under the willow tree. Miss Bells tapped her hoof to the ground and all the ponies snapped their heads up in attention.

"Today, you will be working in groups of three to collect the largest, prettiest bouquet for Mommy Mare's Day.

Poppy looked over at Clover expectantly but Clover turned away in disdain. Normally, the two ponies were an inseparable pair, but lately Clover seemed like she wanted to prove she was the best at everything.

So Poppy jaunted off with Prancer in search of wildflowers. Both ponies were disappointed that Clover did not join, but they were determined to make the most of their day.

Dandelion, Buttercup and Gooseberry set off to search by the pond. Only Clover wanted to work by herself, despite Miss Bells' instructions.

Clover thought to herself . . .
I'm the blue ribbon pony and I always get first place.
I don't want to share the glory and work with
someone else. I'm always the best at everything.

The other pony groups had fun working together finding, collecting, and stashing away the most fragrant and beautiful flowers.

Dandy was particularly good at picking the most delicate flowers, while Prancer was adept at carrying them back to the hollowed out oak tree.

It took Clover twice as long. And working by
herself got boring. She also ran out of ideas
for where to search for special flowers.

Clover longingly gazed at her classmates
frolicking and nickering at each others' jokes.
Why had she thought she'd be better off by
herself? Now, she felt too embarrassed to ask to join.

11

Miss Bells neighed at the ponies that it was time for lunch. Everyone gathered round in the soft cool shade of their beloved willow tree.

As the ponies munched their carrots and oats, Poppy noticed that Clover didn't look so puffed up and full of herself anymore. She had even taken off her first-place ribbon that she liked to wear.

Poppy felt bad for her friend. She could see how her pride was keeping her apart from the other ponies.

"Clover," she called out to her friend, "you collected such pretty flowers—should we combine our flowers together?"

Clover hesitated and almost said no. Then, very quietly, she shyly asked, "You'd still let me join your group?"

All the ponies perked their ears and Prancer stepped forward with a great idea. "If we put all the wildflowers together we could present a grand bouquet to the mare mommies! Would that be okay, Miss Bells?"

Miss Bells' eyes lit up as she gazed at her pupils. "The mare mommies will be so proud of you and how you worked together. You are all super ponies to me!"

CPSIA information can be obtained at www.ICGtesting.com
Printed in the USA
BVOW07s1209230915

419322BV00007B/116/P